I0721932

Saved by the Well

Ivy Hove

WORKBOOK PRESS LLC
187 E Warm Springs Rd,
Suite B285, Las Vegas, NV 89119, USA

Website: https://workbookpress.com/
Hotline: 1-888-818-4856
Email: admin@workbookpress.com

Ordering Information:
Quantity sales. Special discounts are available on quantity purchases by corporations, associations, and others.
For details, contact the publisher at the address above.

ISBN-13:   978-1-954753-77-8 (Paperback Version)
             978-1-954753-78-5 (Digital Version)

REV. DATE: 23/03/2021

All about school bullying

INTRODUCTION

This story highlights some of the effects of bullying or taunting of fresh pupils at a new day or boarding school by senior pupils. Some of the new pupils are rendered emotionally more vulnerable or weaker, just by their dependency on the more senior pupils. They are often initiated into the school routines at a more personal level from the general announcements and notices by the senior pupils, some of who tend to be abusive. On the other hand, a supportive approach to first year pupils' welfare would go a long way to make them feel welcome and accepted into the school fold.

Of course, in other school situations the bullying will go on throughout the year if unreported. Such cases were rare at the Mission school in focus in this book where any taunting of the new pupils would not be tolerated beyond April Fools' Day.

The repressive nature of some senior pupils' actions, often unchecked, impeded the development of trust between pupils and of the new pupils' sense of belonging to the school family.

The main character in this book, Emily, together with other first year pupils, experienced the bullying that would not let up for almost three months. In Zimbabwe, (then Rhodesia) making fun of new pupils at day or boarding school, had become something of a tradition by the 1940s to the 1960s and, probably, with decreasing intensity, beyond these decades. The bullying occurrences were unpredictable and their frequency and intensity depended on the mood and whims of the perpetrator at each encounter.

The fresh pupils soon realised that blowing the whistle only drew the attention of many other tormentors with cheeky and insolent behaviour to them. Soon they learned to endure their humiliation and stress in conspiratorial silence due to fear of reprisals. Fresh pupils were not allowed to be too fresh: they had to be put in their place, to be humiliated by the senior pupils- just like in a game of power. In the most part, the 'initiation', nay, abuse took all sorts of crushing and humiliating forms in effect, though the perpetrators' intentions might not have always been that negative.

The school authorities, including teachers, conscientious as they might be, tended to down-play the unhappy goings-on, if not connive with them altogether in their certainty that they would soon pass. It was not uncommon to hear reports about some teachers who contributed their own sadistic versions on the sly; instead of safeguarding the unfortunate pupils. The bid to protect the good name of the school was likely to lead the staff to deny the existence of bullying at their school; where victims plucked some clout to report to empathetic parents. On the other hand, not many pupils would dare report to their parents the unpleasant treatment meted to them at school unless it was life- threatening. In response, most African parents would sooner urge the child-victim to cope with it as best they could. Understandably so as there were very limited options for most parents after paying the non-refundable school fees- in quite a few cases- procured after selling a precious beast or two.

Apparently, many resilient new pupils did cope or could have just stumbled along without much support and protection to come out of school life with personalities dented for life. It was not easy to know the real extent of any effects of the taunting in such situations.

It is important to mention that in those earlier decades there was a particularly heavy focus on academic education and, in boarding schools; provision for pupils' basic needs, to maintain life and physical health, was also highly prioritized. However, the pupils' psychological and safe care needs hardly received the full extent of the attention they deserved. This practice was due to the fragmented professional values of the time in the field of education. Unfortunately, that perspective ignored the holistic nature of children's needs. On the other hand, the tight budgets by which African schools operated, in that era, would not have allowed much creation of the necessary support services: a situation which still remains in the education sector in independent Zimbabwe today.

In well-resourced countries, schools long started incorporating robust pastoral referral services for the protection, counselling and support of the vulnerable pupils including bullied pupils and the bullies themselves. These services are now being strengthened to support child-victims of cyber- bullying, which has become a global phenomenon across class and age boundaries regardless of educational attainments.

The effects of on-line bulling extend to more critical manifestations: such as self-harming and suicidal tendencies that are on the increase in these affluent countries, according to media reporting. In developing countries, including Zimbabwe, the same challenges may be experienced amidst growing rates today, but remain under reported due to various factors including lack of financial resources. These less resourced countries, like Zimbabwe may still have very limited means of redress.

It is encouraging, though, that currently; unlike the situation in Emily's day, in the 50s; communication between children, their parents and teachers has grown to be much more open. Pupils almost everywhere, including Zimbabwe, are becoming more aware of their rights: - they are becoming more assertive and irrepressible. Not many will suffer from being bullied in silence. But still, the remaining weak and voiceless pupils are a few too many. They must be safeguarded and made to feel welcome throughout their days in school- day or boarding.

Lastly, though the names in this story are fictitious, most incidents narrated, with some embellishments are, on the whole, true. They actually happened.

I

Emily pushed the bucket down the well with her left hand to draw more water. As the bucket filled with the murky water, it became too heavy to pull out.

Although she sensed the likelihood of being pulled down into the well herself, subconsciously she denied it could happen that way. Otherwise, she would have let out a quick deafening scream.

Next thing, she was bobbing under and out of the water, flapping her arms trying helplessly to clutch at the flimsy, slippery straw cascading down from the upper edges of the well. Each time she went down, she gulped more chocking gushes of the filthy water. The more water she swallowed, the deeper she sank like the bucket now resting down the floor of the well.

Emily was not a swimmer and the lack of that coping skill inevitably made a hopeless situation worse. She was getting weaker and weaker and could no longer command her limbs to splash and thrust up out of the well to life. Then she precipitously slid into unconsciousness and, finally, her mind blanked out..........

II

Emily was the first-born child in a family of three boys and two girls aged between three and fourteen years at the time of this incident. Her father, Steven Mandiona, loved all his children and adored and respected his hard-working wife, Sarah. Like most dwellers in Manicaland rural villages the Mandionas mainly depended on the land for their livelihood as peasant farmers.

They grew variety crops: including vegetables, maize, millet, ground-nuts and rapoko for family consumption and for sell to afford poll tax (cash charged adult members of the households as source of revenue for government spending. Poll-tax was then superseded by various forms of taxation), school fees for their children, hospital fees and a host of other life's necessities. In the wake of urbanization growth, barter economy was fast exiting in rural life. In its place, cash economy - the life-blood of western technology - was fast becoming the rule of the day in the economy of Rhodesia.

Once villagers became aware of the value of ready cash in their day today life, they were hooked for good. There was no looking back to the inconveniences of commodity exchanges.

However, attempts to influence some functional traditions, customs and beliefs were met with strong resistance by village communities. It was by dint of their unwavering zeal that the missionaries gradually converted villagers to Christianity. The western missionaries insisted on the importance of serving only one God - the God of Abraham - to gain the heavenly kingdom, thereby escaping the fire of hell. Villagers opted on the former as the prospect of being consumed by eternal fire did not appeal to them much.

With varying degrees of conviction, families and individuals renounced their ancestral gods and dark-related practices. However, it took much longer, if at all, for any outside influences to make much lasting impact on the prescriptions the village communities imposed on women, more so on the girl-child even throughout the forties and early fifties - the period Emily had begun the rapid development into adolescence.

III

Emily had become one of the few girls of the era aspiring to greater heights.

She was a bright and good-looking girl with a vivacious disposition. Sometimes she displayed a rather feisty and wayward nature which left both parents uncomfortable and worried for her future. In those days, for a girl to try and press her point to her parents or any other adult in the family or community, was frowned upon as ill-mannered and disgraceful, especially by the males.

By the time she turned 15, Emily knew her own mind, which could not be said for most of the youths in those times and more so with the girl child. The girl child had very limited room to live a self- determined life outside the customary expectations of the adult members of the African village. Largely, her role was simply to obey and do. So, in this regard Emily was some sort of spirited rebel, one would say, with a cause.

There were a few other girls with supportive families in the village who attended boarding school for higher primary education in various parts of the country. Such girls were increasingly becoming powerful models for the younger ones in the village. But unlike most girls at this stage in the 40s and early 50s, Emily aspired for higher levels in education than was the norm for the majority of the local girls. Her sights extended even as far as training for a viable career which she could not name yet. In later years, she became aware that her passion derived from a desire to make a difference in the life of people in her community and beyond.

The common career pathways for girls, in those decades, were limited to teaching and nursing. Unfortunately, Emily had an extremely dim view of teaching as a career path, to put it mildly. She absolutely hated it. Most girls who had opted for teaching by which, if they managed to complete the course and qualified at all before the heavy-handed pressure of tradition and custom married them off, were sent to teach at village schools. They were to remain country bumpkins still, on the whole.

No, Emily did not want that. With her, teaching went against the grain despite the altruistic benefits accruing from it for younger generations of children to come. On her part, if she should be persuaded to follow the band wagon and decide to marry at all, it had to be for love and from the position of strength.

IV

A few months later Emily was unfortunate enough to contract the malaria bug. Although by then much was known about causes of illnesses from a scientific point of view, the customary beliefs in witchcraft and witch-doctors held much sway.

So it was not surprising that as the disease advanced, the first point of call for consultation and treatment was the famous sekuru Rwata's home- stead. Sekuru Rwata was well-known and respected in the community for his healing powers, real and imagined.

Emily's protestations to her parents against resorting to witch-doctors were firmly ignored. In due course, the classical malaria symptoms of a humming head-ache, soaring and dropping body temperature with copious amounts of sweat and a host of other symptoms manifested themselves and raged on.

Within a week, Emily was getting emaciated, increasingly weak and delirious. Things were not looking good. It was obviously plain, in this instance, Sekuru Rwata or not, traditional medicine had failed to do the trick and this was not lost on Emily as her condition continued to deteriorate. It was now two days into the second week, when her parents and relatives were persuaded to cart her to a Mission rural hospital, twenty miles from the village, for emergency treatment. As luck had it, Dr. Kambiti was around from Marondera town hospital that day.

In a few moments, an intravenous drip of fluids and medication was attached and running through Emily's veins. She had stopped eating and drinking several days before and so she was dreadfully dry, even more emaciated and still confused. The voluntary hospital Chaplin frequently led the family and relatives in powerful prayers of faith and hope during the afternoon visiting hours.

By the end of the third week Emily's eyes and skin began to show some life and her morale had shot up. She had started drinking fluids, eating and retaining food, reaching out from her bed to chat with fellow patients - at first, on beds nearer to hers. Soon she was totting about everywhere in the ward to the bathroom and to return visits.

A fellow patient was heard teasing with a smirk, "You're getting cheeky now, Emily, hey! But it's nice to see you getting better, though." Except for two patients still in the grip of crippling pain and very ill, everyone in the ward including the hospital staff erupted into laughter raising higher the spirit in the ward during that sunny May morning.

Emily could not believe her ears when, on the following Friday, during a morning ward round, the nurse conveyed to her the doctor's message that she could now go home. She was discharged with some medication to complete the course at home.

It so happened that while in hospital, one of the nurses named Gloria, who had attended to her, had made a lasting impression on Emily's mind. This young nurse had a professional flair like a breath of fresh air and a cool demeanour which any young intelligent and spirited girl would not fail to find inspirational.

Back in class, in the middle of a lesson, Emily could not help her mind wandering back to her time in the hospital ward. In spite of willing herself to concentrate, even more so, as she needed to make up for the time lost while she was away ill, she would catch herself at it again. Emily simply cherished the memory of nurse Gloria. She would visualize the energetic nurse gracefully pushing the medicine trolley from one bed to another to administer the contents to one patient, after the other. Sometimes Emily replayed - in her mind- the light chats the esteemed nurse held with patients leaving them cheered. She was indeed phenomenal.

Then that uniform! Emily was simply crazy about the nurse's uniform, crispy and white as snow, topped with starched caps of the same colour always pinned prettily onto their well-groomed hair.

How wonderful to be able to help heal the sick, reassure and make them laugh! Emily thought with a consuming longing.

"That's it then. I'm going to be a nurse, like Gloria when I finish school, working in the wards like nurse Gloria, yes!" Her mind was made-up and not lightly as it turned out.

But soon, Emily realized that with her load of responsibilities in her family it would be nothing but a miracle if she ever achieved a level of performance in standard 6 to proceed to high school.

The demands on her time at home shredded her time to pieces, leaving her little time to even think of her school work, let alone study. There was no way she would be able to give her studies the effort they required for her to make it. She hardly had time to find herself as a developing personality with her home life spent totting from one house chore to another.

Indeed, it was not a situation peculiar to Emily and her family. The practice derived from customary norms of the country then which required girls and their mothers to bear the brunt of the tasks necessary for the wellbeing of the family members. Emily also played a major role in attending to visitors to the family home, who pitched up anytime tired and hungry from distant villages, cities and various growing towns along the railway line in Manicaland or friends of the family in the same village.

The parents would happily assume the sedate role of

entertaining, chatting with the visitors, as it seemed. However, there was a nobler aim, not so obvious, for this apparent tendency for leisure. The parents would be critically monitoring the way Emily went about her tasks, hoping she would give a good impression and not let them down. It was all in the spirit of imparting useful hospitality skills for the girl's benefit then and in her future life. It would not be entirely truthful not to point out that sometimes with parents it was not all about their daughter and her future as it appeared. Indeed, it was also about parental pride in their ability to discipline their daughters and, to lesser degrees, sons, to behave according to the expectations of the traditional society of that era.

"Too many disruptions and disturbances each time I settle down to study and complete my homework!" she thought. Furthermore, her younger sister, Faith - the one after her, had been dispatched to live with her aunt in a village two provinces away and now attended school there. These were some of the arrangements typical between parents and their relatives against which children had no influence at all during those times.

Emily found it all upsetting but, like any other child in the same situation, she had to accept it and soldier on with life. She missed her sister, and would have given anything to have her around if that were possible. They laughed a lot together as they indulged in some child-like pranks and naughty jokes whenever and wherever they could. The main butts of their moments of mischief included teachers at their school and other interesting or funny characters in the village.

Of course, their own parents were not altogether spared. The girls loved to mimic their parents' mannerisms as the duo urged and admonished them to keep on the straight and narrow. But right now, she missed Faith for her capacity and love for work in the family fields.

"I have got to study much more. That is the only way," she

told herself again with grim determination one morning as she served tea to family visitors. Emily would have to juggle between the burdens of her house and school work. She began to use well whatever opportunities that came her way for study and home-work at home and at school. At home, in the evenings, study was by smelly candlelight or oil lamps. Of course, towards examinations, Emily resorted to desperate measures: - studying till midnight after her noisy and younger siblings succumbed to sleep. Often using her father's torch, she slogged on till midnight under her blankets when she was supposed to be asleep. "Could it be?" Emily exclaimed as she registered the passing grade in her end of year report. She was ecstatic and could not resist jumping up and down.

V

The following January Emily found herself at a boarding school forty-miles the other side of the main railway line between Harare and Gweru, then 'Gwelo'. She enjoyed most of her lessons and could see her dream coming true so that all she had to do was give it a good slog.

Sadly, she soon came to realize that the welcome extended to new pupils in their first year by some senior pupils continued to resemble a descent into purgatory, in some instances. The new pupils were referred to as the 'new ones'. Among others the vernacular derogative term in common use at the school was 'magwede'. On its own, the term had no particular bite, if it had any literal meaning at all. It was made to sound much more dreadful on impact to the intended victims - the new comers. The new arrivals shuddered on first being introduced to it. It excited their worst fears - a sure portent of the unpleasant things to come.

Several younger first year pupils often broke down in tears in privacy; missing home, dreading mornings for what torments could be in store for them that day. The taunting continued in spite of repeated warnings against the practice at the morning assemblies by the principal who was also a white-collard reverend of a popular religion. A new pupil cringed at the possibility of bumping into a bunch of those unsmiling faces of the harassing seniors. Of course, not every senior pupil was into the taunting game. Many good-humoured seniors hot for some fun, soothed the sting of their taunting by ending the encounters with some light-hearted jokes.

They would leave in their wake the young pupils doubling with laughter, almost imagining themselves being considered jolly good fellows! Not that they thought less of themselves. Emily had never been so miserable. She was beginning to believe that the taunting of new pupils would never end.

She was nearly sinking into the darkest of despair when a junior prefect named Margaret noticed Emily's sadness as she sat on the steps up to one of the main dormitories.

In those years, it seemed most schools regarded the initiation practice as a given, for a laugh. It resembled some form of weird sport on the part of the senior pupils at the expense of the new pupils. There was nothing much in the way of monitoring to ensure every pupil was physically and emotionally secure. It must have been confusing for some of the younger, delicate first year boarders still trying to make sense of the new complex environment far out of their comfort zone.

Pupils with bullying tendencies had a field day plying their cherished past-time before the deadline to get away with it came. Only a few new comers went through the first three months without a single, crushing brush with the tormenters or bullies at one time or another even those with fierce hulks for friends or home boys/girls to protect them. "Come here, Emily," Margaret gently pulled Emily aside, with one arm on her shoulder and asked why she looked so unhappy. Emily, chest heaving with emotion, explained what was going on.

"Well, has anyone hurt you? I mean hit, pinched or harmed you at all?"

"Oh, no but they do different unpleasant things." "Like what?" Margaret probed further.

"On the day we arrived from home, the first years were compelled to walk a good stretch of the eight- mile distance from the railway station. Some excited senior pupils, boys and girls, had forbidden them to hike a ride on the mule-drawn trailer provided."

"Oh, they do tend to get to extremes," Margaret expressed surprise and some empathy with Emily and encouraged her to continue

"I could not believe it when the new arrivals were only allowed to walk on the road sides over-grown with prickly weeds just for the senior pupils' amusement. Hell broke loose if any of the new comers dared to step back on the clear, untarred road! Can you imagine that, like we were prisoners!" explained Emily.

"How can…. how can they be so cruel?" wondered Margaret.

"We had to step over the prickly wild plants for some time to avoid getting hurt. Still one or two pupils oozed blood from superficial scratches on their feet by the time we were allowed to jump onto the cart," recalled Emily.

"But we never heard that anyone was hurt on the way from the railway station, Emily," Margaret observed. "Of course, no one dared to mention the incidents to anyone, let alone the school hierarchy, for fear of reprisal by the culprits themselves. Some seniors walking on the road even broke into songs full of derisive innuendoes, which I don't want to repeat here, at the expense of new comers," Emily paused. "Some of the suggestible young ones began to wonder if we had transformed into some sort of wild animals with tails," she concluded.

"Life in the Mission has not proved more pleasant either," Lydia, one of first years in Emily's class - who had stopped by intervened. Lydia continued,

"Sometimes a first year is deliberately given wrong directions of where to find things and on getting confused they are derided and made fun of. We have been subjected to verbal put-downs, pushing and shoving including sign and body language conveying dislike and scorn,"

"Some seniors would bump into a new pupil and shout at her to 'look where you go, use your eyes!' and when you try to explain more abuse is hurled at you. No, it is wrong; I can't take any more of this…."

Emily's tears poured over her face again, but she instantly wiped them off with both her hands.

"Ok, ok there's Rose our head-girl. She is coming this way" Margaret warned the two girls to present a cheerful front.

Rose was the head-prefect of the girls' section. She was known for her management flair and so was made head-girl to assist the matron of the two girls' dormitories at the boarding school. She was also known to connive with some of the ruthless tormentors - girls from her village whom she regarded as friends. Rose came tearing by and soon reduced speed as her eyes registered the sad set-up confronting her.

"Oh! What's the matter, why is Emily crying?" Rose directed the question at Margaret. But Emily snapped at the opportunity to explain.

"I am finding life at this place most unbearable. If things remain as bad as they are I might have to seriously think up what to do. I thought the nastiness which new comers are experiencing here would end soon but it goes on forever. No one says anything here in the girls' dormitories," Emily burst out. She continued,

"I was really happy and excited to have made it to this school as a boarder. I was beginning to find myself loving it in class and, thought I could ignore the taunting, but it gets more unpleasant with some seniors when they see you happy as if you're already settled like them. It's as if they're reminding you, 'Not so soon, you cheeky so and so'. Oh…"

Emily burst out crying again. Pupils passing by pretended not to notice or hear a thing. They scuttled past in different directions, their eyes avoiding the scene and the powerful pupil dominating it.

"You'll soon settle down perfectly, Emily. You must have seen it yourself at your village when newly bought cows are left in the kraal or enclosure among other cattle. Are they not given a pretty rough welcome at first before they fully settle in?" Rose, smugly put it to Emily who was quite aware it was an innocent comparison. Rose could never have imagined the fire and heat she had provoked. It was all unexpected and she was completely taken aback. "As you can see sis Rose, new comers are not cows. Now you're calling us cows and dozy cattle of all things. I thought you had come to help. So it's true that underneath that kind face of yours lurks unbelievable spite! How can you be so hard, so unfeeling, uncaring?" Emily screamed eyes aflame with hot anger.

Now that arsenal went home! Rose's cockiness vanished like dew at the break of the bright warm sun. She realized Emily and a few other bright new girls could destroy her in the eyes of the school authorities who had exaggerated regard for her abilities. Throughout Emily's hot outburst Margaret remained silent: - not so sure what was appropriate with Rose.

Instead of a sharp reaction to Margaret's silence as she would normally do when ignored, she held her silence and assumed a contrite attitude. She could have blazed with anger and shouted at Margaret for not openly supporting her. She had been exposed and was recovering from the impact of Emily's torrent of words. It was going to take a long time for Rose to forget this day and Emily's bitter outburst.

When Rose spoke, this time her approach was as persuasive as her voice was quieter and kinder.

"Emily, things will be better as days go by, you'll see. Now that we know what has been going on, we'll try and do everything necessary to protect you and all new pupils from any more unpleasantness. Margaret here will help tell other prefects. How are you feeling now, Emily?" Rose successfully used all her charm to reassure the young girl.

"I would be alright now if only I could trust you would play game and keep your promise. Can I ask you a question?" Emily said.

"Emily you can ask me any question anytime."

"Oh…is it true what I have heard some girls say?" Rose answered the question with one of hers.

"Well, what have you heard?"

"Some girls are saying these goings-on, I mean- the taunting and everything which have made life a virtual hell for most of the first years will get much worse on April's fool day," continued Emily. Beyond that deadline, the senior pupils themselves monitored each other and reported the perpetrators to the prefects or even straight to the matron or House-masters in the boys' section. The first years were now also much vocal but on the whole were now enjoying full acceptance by everyone.

"Normally yes…. people like to mark April 1st by fooling each other for a laugh. A common gag is to tell the dupe that the matron wants to see them at once: - where upon the latter gets paralyzed and dies a thousand deaths before bracing themselves to face their imagined fate. But soon the giggles behind, as they reluctantly march to face their fate, jerk them into realizing what it was really about after all! They would then beat a retreat, twisting with laughter!!

Somewhere down the history of schools, the Fools' Day transitioned into some sort of D- Day with all the attendant unpleasantness for the targeted first years. The taunting is intensified during that day," Rose paused.

"And from 2nd April there will be no more of this nonsense- this unnecessary initiation, ever?"

"That's right, except for ordinary bullying here and there found at most schools anytime in the school year which is strictly forbidden. Actually, there should be no taunting at all at any time inflicted upon new arrivals at any school, boarding or day whatsoever. But somehow, the tradition dies hard," Rose started to offer a placatory explanation. "Is that so?" wondered Emily with some warmth towards the Head-girl.

Rose continued, "There have been cases where some parents have had to relocate their children to schools they believed to be safer, only to be disappointed. Last year a child aged 14 begged her mother to bring her back to this school. She is still here, happy and doing very well in standard 4."

"Amazing, but what happened to the bullies. Are they still here too?" Emily interjected quizzically.

"What do you think? Of course, they are still around treating him with love, like their younger brother," Rose replied.

"Isn't that wonderful" Exclaimed Emily.

"Yes, some progress has been made in the past six years I have been here. I can see it eventually disappearing all together with each passing year as more pupils and their parents get brave enough to challenge it," answered Rose quite convincingly. It was difficult to know whether Rose was sincere and contrite or just play-acting to paint a glowing impression in Emily's eyes.

"Well, that is encouraging," put in Emily with even more enthusiasm.

"However, I remember two of a few cases which did not have such a happy ending," said Rose. "Well, what happened?" Emily wanted to know.

"In the first one, two pleasant girls were given a hard time when it became known they came from a police camp. It so happened that some senior boarders had close relatives in prison. The reasoning or justification clutched on then was that the girls' fathers must have had some part in the incarceration of these pupils' criminal relatives. There also were boarders anxious that their relations leading criminal lives might sooner or later be nabbed and be made to face a similar fate. The question often thrown at the girls was, "Why did your father send my uncle, brother or aunt to Harare Central Prison (the main prison in Zimbabwe)?"

The girls were never allowed to explain themselves as volleys of verbal abuse and threats were unleashed with guffaws of laughter."

"Well, I can imagine." Emily empathized.

"Most of the abusers neither knew which jail a relation was sentenced to nor, if they did, were they all that concerned about them. Towards the end of February, the two girls were withdrawn by their parents for their safety and never returned to school the following term. The other incident with much currency was about a boy in early adolescence who quoted the threats made to him by his abusers in a letter to his parents. The threats were thrown at the boy whenever he refused to continue being a little servant for the bullies who forced him to do menial tasks the culprits found inconvenient. The threats were so blood-cuddling that the parents did not waste time to withdraw their son from the school before anything untoward happened to him," Rose said. She continued to narrate "The boy's school career was ruined, as from then on, he refused to be a new pupil at any school. Rumour has it that he became a street-kid and he was saved by a Charity from America which trained him to become a highly skilled mechanic. The young man ended up one of the wealthiest business man of Zimbabwe. Since there was never a name attached to this story, its veracity has been very difficult to prove."

"I feel much better now, Rose. I'm sure I will be able to cope now: I'll try anyway." At this stage Emily was truly convinced about the changes in Rose's attitude and did believe she would try her best to help the first year pupils from any more abuse.

In her heart, Rose knew she would be game and step up to changing her reputation for the better.

Of course, it was not going to be easy as she had to attend to many things including her own studying.

VI

All throughout March, Margaret made sure Emily and other new pupils were protected whenever she and other prefects could. But as they attended different classes, there would be times Emily and other new comers would be exposed to abuse by some seniors. Besides, Margaret and other girls in her position had their share of prefect duties to carry out. Emily had to admit that she and other new girls were on the whole much happier than what pertained before she shocked and frightened Rose with her protests.

But whatever comfort she now felt was dampened by the thought of the imminence of April 1st. What was likely to happen to her in the absence of Margaret? By the dawn of 31st March her dread of April 1st had become an obsession. She had also experienced a few horrific nightmares arising from her anxieties about the fateful day. Only the confirmation that the day would mark the end of the harassment and taunting gave her hope and some relief.

However, all first years could not forget what miseries the dawn of April the 1st was known to bring. The heart-rending reality was that the dawn of day was already around the corner. It had to come to pass. It was not as if the whole bunch of first years were excluded from the rest of pupils to go through hell. Indeed, there were light moments here and there when the new pupils found themselves on their own heading for classes, other school projects or tasks allocated by the head girl.

Of course, they would grab such opportunities to share common unhappy experiences, laughing out loud together in a spirit of comradery as common victims. Sighting any of the bullies approaching, the merriment would cease instantly.

Nor did the bullying take place all the time. It varied with circumstances; days could pass with just an incident here and there. Then as one began to feel settled there could be one bullying incident after another, by the same or different pupils, like that, unpredictably.

That year, the school's gardening programmes or horticultural lessons, which normally began in early March, were deferred to the end of the same month. The dam, two miles from the mission school, was still under construction and so gardens for horticultural lessons had to be situated near a river or existing deep water well. Plans to install health and safety measures around water sources had been abandoned as soon as the dam construction became a reality.

The monumental engineering project required a colossal amount of funding for hire of heavy machinery and other construction paraphernalia to complete. The extension of water pipes to the gardening sites from both boys' and girls' dormitories was still far in the future.

It was assumed by Mrs. Mutangi, the gardening instructor, that since Emily came from a rural background she would be familiar with drawing water from such open sources as rivers and other precarious water wells. While that assumption was true, villagers back at Emily's home had long put into place security measures around water sources after nasty experiences of women and girls drowning while fetching water.

So on the afternoon of March 31st, on a Friday, Emily and other pupils worked busily to prepare beds to transplant vegetables of their choice. The full-time manual labour from surrounding villages employed by the mission for odd maintenance jobs would water the plants during the coming school holiday in April.

Emily was already quite good at gardening and field tasks. It was quite clear from the way she went about on her patch that she had had some exposure and did not need much guidance. As a result, she was one of the last ones to start watering her expertly transplanted seedlings. Mavis, the prefect, was assisting Mrs Mutangi, the gardening instructor that afternoon. She had a few other important tasks to carry out apart from work on her patch. Right now, she was advising one of the youngest girls how to execute neat, symmetrical corners at both ends of her oblong vegetable bed.

Normally, Mavis made sure she was present when Emily made the trip to the well. Not that she doubted Emily's ability to draw the water using one of the buckets provided for the purpose that afternoon. But, somehow, something about this first year gave Mavis cause for concern. Emily had that over-confident dash in most of her actions. The behaviour made Mavis uneasy; fearing the first year might act impulsively and get into some scrape of some sort.

Emily had not taken well to Mavis escorting her to the well. She simply resented the attention she considered unwarranted and humiliating. On the other hand, she was not ready for another outburst with a prefect when her confrontation with Head- girl, Rose, was still a subject of much talk at the mission. Therefore, she endured the loss of face in silence for a while. On her part, Mavis had no idea that negative comments were already being thrown at the first year about her apparent need for help in using the well.

VII

Emily proceeded to the well alone, confident she would be alright and at the same time hoping to impress Mavis with her independence. The water well was about hundred and fifty yards from the gardening site. It was hidden from view behind a towering ant-hill in most part covered from view by swaying, leafy shrubs and brambles so that no one could see from the garden what went on at the well. Still dangling her empty water bucket and humming an indistinct tune, Emily strode determinedly without looking back. She was not fazed on realising there was no one else in sight at the well. That often happened, even back home at her village, and so she did not make much of it. But as she neared the water well, she suddenly stopped in her tracks, killed the humming, her eyes taking in the condition on the edge of the well where pupils stood as they drew the water.

The usual green grass surrounding the well was now matted down with greyish mud, beaten down by the girls' feet as they drew the water, it looked slippery all around. A shuffle in the thickets led Emily's eyes to a grey-green lizard scampering away from her as she advanced to the well.

It was not a green mamba as she had feared. The thought of any type of snake made her cringe with dread. However, with other snakes it was possible to be warned by their colours which were distinct from the green grass background. In an unfortunate incident at Emily's home village, sometime back, a teenage cattle herder was found dead - prostrate on the grass in the green marshes and had only the time to call out 'green mamba' while he turned almost jet black in his few last moments on earth.

He had not spotted the insidious creature, silently preparing its deadly poison, before it lurched onto his ankle and, just as instantly, slithered into the green nothingness around the ill-fated cattle herder ; not before the adolescent had identified it by the colour of its rear-end - its tail. But it was still to no avail to save his life. It was, as the saying goes: too little too late. The sharp-eared old man, who got the muffled call as he advanced to the expiring youth, alerted the other villagers about the tragedy. Well, that was some years ago.

But now here she was, she had to get to the well now. So with aggressive determination, she took a giant stride forward and knelt by the well, on a surface less muddy.

She found she had to strain and bend right down precariously to reach the reeking water. Of course, she would not call for help as that would provide the senior girls with more ammunition to laugh at her, if not this evening, the next day. "I cannot go back there without the water," she thought. She cast the bucket into the well. Then as she strained to pull the bucket out, the unexpected happened: - she toppled into the gapping well.

VIII

When Emily came to, twenty minutes later, she was perplexed to find herself almost surrounded by anxious faces, which instantly broke into unexplainable cheer. In a blur, she could only make out that she was the center of some attention. The dampness of her clothes caused her to shiver.

The choking cough assailed her for a few flitting moments again.

"What has happened to me? Why am I so wet? Have I been sick or something?" She spluttered, talking to herself. She attempted to heave herself up and stand on her giddy feet; only to wince with pain, her right hand on her chest. She swooned and flopped back prostrate on the ground. She had fainted.

"Now, now steady on, Emily. Come Mavis let's lift her onto the wheel borrow and rush her to the mission clinic," the instructor tersely beckoned Mavis to assist as she felt the racing pulse. Betty, an assistant prefect present, with several senior pupils, were soon carefully rushing the barely conscious Emily to the clinic.

On their way Mavis quickly explained how she had to take a plunge into the well to rescue Emily.

"I should have been with her at the well. But being Emily, she went ahead alone," Mavis started to explain apologetically.

"Oh well, it's not possible for anyone to be everywhere at the same time," comforted Mrs. Mutangi before she strode to feel Emily's pulse once more and supported her through a short paroxysm of chocking and coughing.

"As soon as I noticed her absence I ran to the well.

As I maneuvered the anthill, I heard the sound of colossal grunts, panicked splashed and bubble- bursts; like someone was struggling under and out of water and then it clicked!" She put both arms round her nose and shivered with a shudder as she tried to recall the series of events.

"Go on," urged the gardening instructor.

"I didn't waste any time, Lydia heard me yell as I plunged into the well to save Emily. In an instant, almost like a miracle, she had dragged the limp Emily to a drier place a patch- a pace away from the mud round the well," Mavis said with much gesticulating. She continued, "In a split second I heaved myself out of the well fitfully straining to remember my First Aid,"

"But you did remember," complimented the instructor with much admiration for the brave pupil.

"No, not at first I almost went into fits with anxiety; then all of a sudden, the procedure, some of it anyway, flashed back to memory. Then, positioning Emily's head accordingly, I fell to. I think she will be alright," Mavis assured the instructor.

"Thank you so much for your bravery. Imagine what would have happened if you had not acted quickly. Let's all go home girls all of us," the instructor called out as the two hurried to catch up with the wheel burrow.

"Emily must have swallowed lots of water in the well," the instructor observed.

"Definitely, she spewed out oceans of it which was good for her recovery," Mavis answered, bubbling inside with elation that she had been able to save Emily's life single-handedly. There was so much whispering to that effect already among fellow-pupils as they cast furtive glances dripping with awe and admiration at the heroin.

At the clinic, the Rhodesian nurse, Mrs. Tamuka detained Emily for more observations and treatment. She also instructed her to take lots of clean fluids so as to flush out the well filth from her system. Emily was transferred to the dormitory sickroom with instructions to continue with the treatment regime prescribed.

On his way from the Sunday church services, the principal, accompanied by the nurse and the matron of the girls' section, visited Emily in the girls' sick bay. Though still limping slightly from the accident, the Matron had now been pronounced fit for work by doctors at the hospital in Gweru and seemed to be coping, as expected, with support.

"There she is. Thank God, she looks better than I'd feared," the principal observed as he headed straight towards Emily, who was resting on the simplest type of bedding facility the mission could afford.

"Well, how are you feeling, Emily? Mrs. Tamuka here assures me things are looking positive, she has done a good job. Thank you" the principal added his eyes turning to the humble nurse.

"Well, the cough has subsided, I am getting less feverish and I cannot eat yet because I feel sick at the sight of food. I think I'll soon be alright, Sir," replied Emily with a shy smile of respect for the Rev. Just before the nurse was about to expand on Emily's condition the principal cut in,

"Matron, have you any idea how deep that well is- the well at the garden?"

"Absolutely, no idea, Sir. But now that I remember, I think it is many feet deep, but I can't remember the exact figure," the matron replied.

"Twenty-three feet," shrieked the principal, baring his gapped white teeth with emphasis, while rubbing at his well-trimmed goatee. He proceeded to point out that the mission authorities in the country and abroad had records proving the existence of such a well and how it came about.

"Who could have done such a dreadful thing to the mission farm? "The nurse asked with surprise, as she fumbled for something in one of the drawers of the medicine cupboards which had seen better days and was giddy on the floor.

The principal continued, "I have not had sight of any records myself, but my predecessor gave me a snippet account of the well's origin, quite interesting. He said that during military drills in the early 1940s soldiers, recruited for the Second World War, blasted a detonator in the vast grassland around that area as part of their training. Since then, the resulting crater always contains water in its depths but in spring the water comes up to the brim due to the summer and spring rains.

We have never had any such incidents as the one which occurred on Friday. But then in the 19- 40s, pupils were comparatively much older almost adult by the time they walked to school for the first time; these years the starting ages continue to get younger. Anyway, something has to be done about that well to make it safe for use and soon. Otherwise one day- one unlucky day......." The principal concluded and sighed in desperation, shaking his head inwardly wondering when the dam would be completed at that snail-slow pace.

The following Monday morning, three of Emily's first year friends burst into the small dormitory sickroom, faces sparkling with excitement, ready to go for classes.

"Emily! You look so much better today," exclaimed Lydia.

"Oh, how was it on April Fool's day? I heard some commotion: a lot of giggling, whining, exclamations and complaints outside somewhere but I was still unwell and unable to find out what was happening." Emily said.

"It was worse than we ever imagined. But now it's over. Lucky you!" Lisa said with a lowered voice, like a teasing sneer.

Then with a smile which soon broke into a mischievous giggle, she edged nearer to Emily to share some of the taunting of the whole day of Saturday- April Fool's Day. The patient was sitting towards the edge of the bed dangling her legs, her right arm resting on her pillow, apparently in deep thought.

Then she raised her head and with a ghost of a smile murmured, "You know what, as I slowly regained my consciousness on the wheel-burrow, on the way to the school clinic, one of the dreaded bullies, Taku, loudly made a weird remark. I hope to God they don't think the well incident was intentional."

"Oh, that terror! Don't mind the lot of them. But what did she say?" Lydia demanded, thereby, contradicting herself.

For a moment Emily struggled with her emotions in silence - her eyes swimming in tears, an expression between weeping and smiling.

Then she revealed that Taku confided in Ngoni that she, Emily, was now unreachable for the tribulations of the 1st of April both had planned for her. Ngoni, Taku's friend, and one of the most feared teasers had a small and scrawny physique with a kind pretty face that belied her sadistic nature.

According to Emily Ngoni, assuming she, Emily, was still unconscious had shot in a curt response.

"We don't know that for certain, do we? She might still be reachable. But come to think of it, on second thought, we would be better advised not to mess about with that scream. Did you hear how she shrieked at the mighty Rose? She literary cut her down to size, incredible hey! Better let sleeping dogs lie till eternity. That's what I say." Emily was pleasantly surprised as she had no idea her outburst at Rose earlier in the year had shaken more bullies than the head girl herself.

"Good! You got them, Emily. Cowards!" Lydia hugged Emily amidst ecstatic shouting and triumphal giggles, by the other girls. Emily then took a deep breath and concluded her story with unbelievable humility.

"Well, the way I felt before the well incident, I could have given the world to escape the dreaded April Fool's Day. Yet, right now I'm unable to jump for joy that I am alive. I could have easily died that day. Anyway, I'm glad the strife is over now, thank God."

Emily never forgot her lonely struggle down that dark, dark garden well.

Ivy Hove

Ivy Hove, a retired social worker, was born in Zimbabwe. Presently, she lives in Birmingham, UK. She has three grown up children who have long flown the nest.

Ivy has always found much pleasure in reading but, lately, has embarked on creative writing.

Visit www.ivyswritings.com to connect with Ivy Hove and for more information about her writing.

www.ingramcontent.com/pod-product-compliance
Lightning Source LLC
Chambersburg PA
CBHW060806210726
48292CB00013B/1897